# The Seal Prince

retold by Sheila MacGill-Callahan

pictures by Kris Waldherr

*Dial Books for Young Readers* New York

## Author's Note

*This story was told to me by my father,*
*Patrick MacGill,*
*who came from Glenties in the Donegal Highlands of Ireland.*
*He said it was told to him by his father. I have taken a storyteller's liberty*
*and added details of my own. Dad did not identify the Scottish island.*
*I set the story on the Isle of Skye because I have loved the name "Skye"*
*ever since I first heard "The Skye Boat Song" and dreamed*
*romantic dreams about "...the lad who was born to be king."*
*It is an old tale and exists in many versions. I hope this version*
*will appeal to a new generation of readers and serve as an introduction*
*to the treasure house of Irish and Scottish stories.*

Published by Dial Books for Young Readers
A Division of Penguin Books USA Inc.
375 Hudson Street / New York, New York 10014

Text copyright © 1995 by Sheila MacGill-Callahan
Pictures copyright © 1995 by Kris Waldherr
All rights reserved
Designed by Amelia Lau Carling
Printed in Hong Kong
First Edition
1  3  5  7  9  10  8  6  4  2

Library of Congress Cataloging in Publication Data
MacGill-Callahan, Sheila.
The seal prince / retold by Sheila MacGill-Callahan;
pictures by Kris Waldherr.   p.   cm.
Summary: When it comes time for Grainne, the beautiful
daughter of the lord and lady of Skye, to marry, she rejects
the island suitors to be with Deodatus, a seal-man
she once rescued from death.
ISBN 0-8037-1486-6 (trade).—ISBN 0-8037-1487-4 (lib.)
[1. Fairy tales. 2. Folklore—Scotland.]  I. Waldherr, Kris, ill.  II. Title.
PZ8.M175967Se 1995
398.21'09411—dc20   [E]   93-16248   CIP   AC

*The art for each picture was made with watercolor paints and colored pencils.*
*The paintings were then color-separated*
*and reproduced as red, yellow, blue, and black halftones.*

For Michael, Christina, and Brian Callahan
with all my love
S. M. C.

For Patrice Silverstein and Michael Natale
K. W.

In the days that were, a daughter was born to the lord and lady of Skye, to comfort them in their old age. They called her Grainne, which means grace, for when she was laid in her mother's arms, her mother felt the tiny fingers grasp her own and said, "This is a joy I never expected; she is the grace of my later years."

Grainne grew to be as good as she was beautiful. The grim castle by the sea was brightened with her songs and laughter. The lord and lady gained new strength from her coming, and they refused her nothing.

On her eighth birthday she was playing on the shore while her mother watched. There she found a baby seal half buried in the sand and unable to move because he was pinned down by a huge piece of timber. Grainne pushed and pulled, but was unable to free him. She called to her mother, whose strength was also unequal to the task. Finally, with the aid of some fishermen who were mending their nets nearby, the timber was lifted clear.

The flipperling lay panting on the strand. There was a long, bloody gash down his back and he was so exhausted that he was unable to move toward the water.

Grainne folded her arms around his neck and was whispering softly in his ear, when suddenly there was a great roiling of the

water and two large seals heaved out of the surf. With one on each side they drew the little seal between them, and vanished beneath the sea.

Exactly a year later the seal, grown much larger now, appeared again and seemed to be waiting for Grainne on the strand. Every year thereafter he came back on her birthday and stayed with her from the rising to the setting of the sun. Grainne held these days in her heart.

On her eighteenth birthday she saw her parents with grown-up eyes and realized they were old and had as yet no plans for her wedding or for what would happen to Skye when they were gone. So when she came to the beach at dawn to wait for the rising of the sun, her mood was somber and full of foreboding.

There was a young man on the beach. He was tall and dark, clad in a simple white tunic, and at his throat flashed the gem-inlaid

golden torque of a great prince. Beside him on the sand lay a
dark-gray mantle.

"Well met, stranger," said Grainne. "I am the Princess Grainne,
daughter to the lord and lady of Skye. And you are . . . ?"

"Do you not know me, lady?" He turned his dark eyes upon her
and she saw they were the eyes of her old friend the seal.

Then a cold shiver touched Grainne's spine, for she had heard
the stories that were whispered around the night fires. Stories of
how creatures of the sea, the seal-men and -women, lured unwary
mortals beneath the waves. Some said it was to a cold death, and
some said they were taken by their lovers to Tir nan Og, the bright
land of the forever young.

But Grainne had known and loved the seal for eleven birthdays
now. She could not believe that he, owing her his life, could wish
her ill. She laid her hand in his.

"I know you well, so we are doubly well met. Tell me by what name to call you."

"My mother calls me Deodatus, for in the tongue of a people far from here it means 'gift of God.' Come with me beneath the sea. I will show you wonders that your landlocked mind cannot even imagine." He picked up the gray cloak from the sand and moved to throw it around her shoulders.

Grainne stepped back sharply. Clearly etched in her mind were the warnings in the old tales. Once a seal-man had thrown his cloak over a mortal, she was doomed to follow him beneath the waves and give her will and her future into his hands. But her heart was breaking with love for him, and there was nothing she wanted so much as to follow where he led.

A sapling of the rowan tree, the surest guard against all magic, light or dark, grew near the shore. Grainne stood behind it as a shield. "I cannot come, Deodatus. My parents are old and I am all they have. To go with you would mean their death. And," she drew herself to her full height, pride mixed with sorrow on her face, "I am the next lady of Skye. My first duty is to my people."

That night there was a great birthday feast at the castle. A special guest was the son of the king of Iona who had come to press his suit for Grainne's hand in marriage. He was a tall man, handsome and gentle in manner, but Grainne had no eyes for him. All she could think of was Deodatus.

Year followed year. Every year there was a feast, and every year a host of new suitors sought Grainne's hand. Every year on her birthday Grainne went at dawn to survey the beach from behind the rowan, which had now grown to a large tree. And every year Deodatus stood waiting on the beach.

On the morning of her twenty-fifth birthday her father called her to him. "Do not go to the beach today. It is time that you chose a husband. I have not pressed you for all these years, but my time is running out and I would like to see a grandchild before I die. Choose, or I will choose for you, for you have spurned all the princely suitors. And dearly though I love you, I'll wed you to the first man who crosses my door."

The sun was well up in the heavens when Grainne reached the beach. Without seeking the protection of the rowan tree, she ran across the sand and threw herself into Deodatus's arms.

"Take me," she cried, "for my father will give me in marriage today whether I will or no, and I cannot bear to live without you."

"Go back to the castle, Grainne. For I too have my honor, and I will not take a woman from her duty. Had you brothers and sisters, all would be easy. Go now, before I lose my resolve, for my heart is near to breaking."

That night at the birthday feast the high table was crowded, but not with suitors. Word had gone out that the princess of Skye spurned any man who asked for her hand.

At midnight the lord of Skye rose to his feet. "My daughter brings as dower the Isle of Skye, which is hers by right of blood.

Since she has not seen fit to choose any of the princes who have wooed her these many years, I offer her in marriage to the man who by sunup tomorrow can bring me the largest catch of fish."

There was a moment of stunned silence, now broken by rushing feet as all the single men present ran for their boats.

The rising sun showed a trail of men struggling up the path from the beach, bowed under the weight of their nets.

First came Manus whose net was near to bursting with silvery herring; Manus had hands like hams, bowed legs, and a wart on the end of his nose. Then came Frang. His net was dragging behind.

Frang was tall and skinny, he had a pointed head and a pointed nose that dripped. Hot on their heels came Barra, Art, and Pol, each uglier than the other. Men did not stay single long on Skye. The ones who could find no lass to marry them had to be very poor specimens indeed.

Finally all were assembled. The great hall stank of fish, and Frang was the winner. Although she was shrinking inwardly, Grainne gathered up what was left of her pride and advanced to take the hand of Frang, when there was a commotion at the door.

A tall man wrapped head to foot in a gray cloak stood in the shadow of the arch.

"I have come to compete for the hand of the princess," he announced in a loud voice. "It is my understanding that she is being given away for a load of dead fish."

The stinging contempt in his voice brought a flush to the cheek of the lord of Skye. "She has had many years to choose a different fate," he retorted. "Who are you? Have you brought your fish to be judged? I have given my word."

"And I have brought my fish," said the stranger. He moved into the light and Grainne saw it was Deodatus. He made a sign to those behind him. A line of tall men clad head to toe in dark-gray mantles filed into the room. Each carried a net filled to bursting. They emptied the nets on the floor in a great pile, far larger than any other. In each fish's mouth was a softly glowing gem.

Grainne took Deodatus's hand and faced her father proudly. "This is Deodatus, prince of the Seals and my own true love."

The lord of Skye's face turned ashy. "A seal-man? Nay, I was angered, Daughter, but I cannot give you to such a one."

Now it was Grainne's turn. "But you could sell me to such as these for a load of fish. That is not love, Father. I will go with Deodatus and find the love that has waited for me all these years."

"No." Deodatus slipped off his cloak and handed it to Grainne. "Hold tight to that and keep it safe for me. As long as you hold to my sealskin, I cannot dive back beneath the waves and live. I will dwell with you on Skye until our oldest son can take over the lordship. That, my lord, is my thanks to Grainne and your lady-wife who took pity years ago on a hurt baby seal."

"And then, my love?" asked Grainne softly.

"Then we two will go beneath the waves to the land of Tir nan Og, where we will live until the end of time."

So they were married and danced on the shore to the song of the seal-people. As time went on, they were blessed with a son and a daughter who were good, wise, and beautiful.

On their son's eighteenth birthday Grainne found Deodatus on the beach looking out to sea.

"It is time," she said as she drew the cloak over their shoulders. He took her hand and led her into the water and they were never seen again.

From then on, the people of Skye took their newborn babies to the edge of the sea and laid them for a moment in the waves to ask the blessing of Grainne and Deodatus. And many a fisherman's life has been saved when his boat has foundered by two great seals who bear him safely to the shore.